Felicia Williams

Seduction Games: *How to unleash the Freak*

Illustrations by: Roger L. Patterson Jr.
ISBN-13: 978-0-692-04259-5

The Boudoir Boss Presents

Seduction Games
How to unleash the Freak

Author Felicia M. Williams

Illustrations By Roger L. Patterson Jr.

Dedication

This manual is dedicated to all the lovers in a current sexual slump who are looking for creative ways to spice up the bedroom.

This manual aims to assist in a fun, playful way by bringing the passion and freakiness back to relationships that have let life get in the way.

This manual is for the recent divorcée who must get back out there and start a new adventure of sexual liberation.

This manual is for any woman who has lost her libido and is determined to get it back by any means necessary!

Table Of Contents

Foreplay

Foreplay stimulates the mind, which in turn controls the body. Although we won't go into all the technical, biological, or medical terms behind it, it is important to note from the outset that the act of foreplay has been proven to be the best way to prepare the mind and body for sex.

That said, buckle up and let's have some fun. Prepare to be driven deep into a mind-blowing zone filled with tips on how to achieve the best of foreplay and get fully aroused and enthusiastic about sex.

Your mind has the capability to be driven to a different place—a more pleasurable one—and if you follow the simple-yet-fun instructions, be assured that you will have countless rippling orgasms.

Having spoken to many people as an Adult Party Consultant, I came to the conclusion that the main issue is monotony, defined as the *lack of variety and interest or tedious repetition and routine*. The major complaint from concerned individuals was that they did the same old thing, time after time. They were confounded. They did not know how to get their partners to change or how to change themselves—how to try new, totally different techniques.

Listening ardently to them, I learned every single time that women of a certain age or women who have been in a relationship for a long time are as bored as fuck in the sex

department! I was quick to mention this to the women that I spoke to.

"There! I said it!" a great partygoer screamed, admitting I was right with my assumption. A look of relief settled on her face. For her, the party (aka therapy session) provided a major breakthrough–the kind that suddenly enlightened her about a problem she had been confronted with for a long time but had been too stubborn to accept.

I have been taught that the first step to fixing a problem is admitting that there is indeed a problem. Many women are suffering in silence because they do not want to hurt their partner's feelings.

To change the monotony of your sexual encounters, you must be creative and willing to explore new tactics that keep both parties looking forward to being intimate. Let "intimacy" suggest the ability to be in each other's arms with endless moans and gasps, with a slow, provocative exploration of each other's skin and sensitive sexual organs.

The idea isn't that you should jump right into sexual acts that you know little about. I mean, *Fifty Shades of Grey* was an erotic and fascinating book but I don't suggest going straight to gags and floggers. Foreplay, in my opinion, should be a fun, flirty way to engage your partner's mind with what is to come. Get your body to steam with want. Get his head filled with images of the endless climax that is soon to envelop his crotch. In a nutshell, a simple term to define foreplay would be "sexual teasing."

If I ask most people what they do to get down to the act of sex, most will probably say that they start by kissing. If you have been fucking someone–yes, you read right! I used the F-word. Let's be real, shall we?–for as long as you have been of age, then you pretty much know the mating game: kiss, suck, and then fuck.

The goal is to teach those suffering from mundane sexual experiences that there are other ways to have sex—you too can experience in your partner's arms an adventure that will leave both of you simultaneously breathless and euphoric.

I am not an expert; you might want to get rid of that assumption. I just know how to make my sexual encounters more memorable for my partner. And I can tell you that once I changed my mindset on certain choices, my partner changed to keep up with me.

Foreplay is a two-way thing. Don't ever think it is simply about your sexual prowess or that of your partner. It is about being able to tease each other so well, you can stare straight into each other's eyes and know that you want nothing else than to uniformly reach a heart-throbbing climax.

Importance Of Foreplay

Keep in mind that there are no rules to foreplay because sex should not make either you or your partner tense. When you first attempt the following games in the bedroom, don't stress over them.

The rules simply are there are no rules. Be creative. Implement ideas that you think you and your partner can enjoy. And when you notice that you do not like a game, modify it into something you both can have total satisfaction from, no matter how simple it might seem. The steps are laid out for your fun and amusement, but it is up to you to make sure they fit your particular situation.

What I need you to do first is to create an alter ego. An alter ego—another you—can play any role that you desire. You can become the wild cat woman who will fulfill every kinky fantasy of your lover. You can also become the meek maid who will do anything subservient in order to get your thighs shuddering with delight when your lover dominates every inch of your sensitive skin.

Creating an alter ego helps take your normal self out of the picture. Your normal self will not heighten your sense of sexiness; isn't the goal to bring sexy back in a fun, playful experience?

So, create a personality that is your total opposite. If you are generally a soft-spoken kitten type, then you must create

an alter ego that is bold and brash. Adding dominance to your experience will excite your partner because he cannot imagine you as an aggressor and that's the whole goal. Changing into an atypical role will become such a turn on, your partner will be unable to wait to see what you do next.

Using certain commands during intercourse will add to the experience. Of course, do well to notice that I used the word "commands" because you are the commander-in-chief and whatever you say, goes. Do Not deviate from the role! Be forceful with your commands: when you say "Sit and watch" or, "Do not take your eyes off me," say it like you mean it. When you think sexy, you feel sexy, and that sexy vibe is conveyed to your partner properly.

Ask any stripper or porn star how they do what they do and many will tell you that they embody a character who gives the performance of an erotic sex goddess. You will find many men ogling them. Some become so fixated that they dip their hands through their waistband and squeeze their cocks as hard as they can.

There's a simple shortcut to feeling like a sex goddess: lingerie! And contrary to popular opinion, you don't need expensive pieces. Do you really think your partner cares what the lacy panties or bras cost? No! All he cares about is how it looks and how long before it comes off.

An inexpensive silk, satin, or lace number is sexy. Providing it isn't stained or has seen better days, an everyday, clean matching bra and panty set or a tube sock is also sexy. But your confidence while wearing the outfit is the real key.

Throughout foreplay, you must remember your goal—to make him make you climax—perhaps in a way you and your partner never have before.

The Games Of Foreplay

With foreplay, I personally think lovers should start off slow and then subsequently ease into something a little more erotic. So, for now, I'll explain the first foreplay interaction game, which I call "The Sticky Note Hoe."

The Sticky Note Hoe

The name says everything about what this is, doesn't it? The Sticky Note Hoe is a simple game of scribing the kind of kinky or shameless slut that you want your alter ego to become. The only tools you need are a sticky note pad and a color marker and, while you're already thinking this could be rather boring, I should explain that we are taking scribing beyond the typical notch.

Your alter ego would never take the easy route, so you should dig deep into the freaky part of your brain and use your imagination. If possible, listen to your clenching pussy and learn whatever makes your breasts or clit tingle.

Take a minute and use the worksheet provided in the back of the manual. Fill in the blanks of some potential freaky task that you want to be done to you.

Go wild with this!

It could be that you want a hardcore penetration of your pussy. Perhaps the idea is to cross-dress and roleplay each other's genders while you're tearing off each other's attire.

Each sticky note should reflect an individual fantasy or request. The fun part is to decide where you will strategically place them. Personally, I prefer the parts of the body we normally neglect, such as the back of your neck, your forehead, the back of your thigh, the tip of your nose. Let your imagination lead you to your most erotic zone.

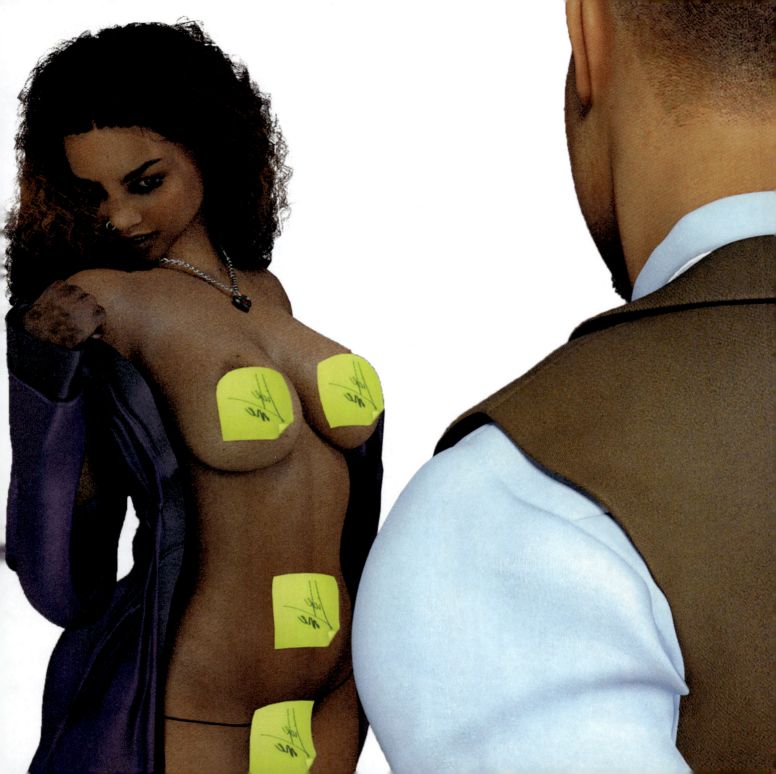

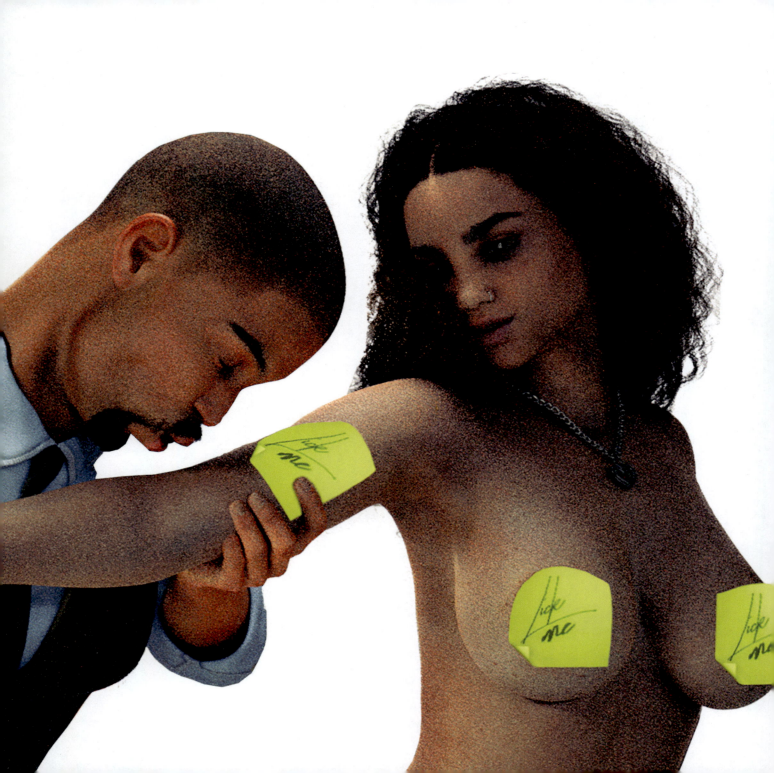

Of course, don't forget the most sensual parts of your body. Certainly, you can also put sticky notes in more obvious places like on a nipple or your butt cheek or even your belly button! Your nipples don't become taut because you are hungry or pissed at someone. They become so pointed and sensitive because of your imagination—because of the simple touch from your partner that has been able to fill your mind with expectations of a growing climax.

Always remember: the only rule is that there are no rules. The Sticky Note Hoe game is just a tool to enable you to have all the fun you could ever imagine.

Masturbation Climax Manifestation

Try saying this three times in a row while chewing gum and I bet you can't go without hurting your tongue.

No matter what you have been told, masturbation is a great foreplay experience. It is an aspect of foreplay that can never be diminished. It prepares the individual, as well as their partner, for parts of their bodies that could easily dig deep in their most climatic zone. It's also an easy way of showing your partner how he can please you, and suggesting you can do the same to him.

I masturbate and I don't mind sharing this news with people. Neither should you, because *everyone* does it, just in different forms. Sharon, the friend you think doesn't masturbate, might not use dildos but she does touch herself in the shower or bathtub.

There is nothing sexier than watching someone in a climatic state. It releases endorphins within you and anyone who watches can't help but have a reaction of mental gratification that excites the physical. In the instance that this happens with your partner, do not limit your imagination or your erotic thoughts.

The element of anticipation is often the perfect way to prepare your partner for the best sexual experience. For instance, send him a text and advise him of the time and place to meet. The text could be a short note such as:

It is very important that you meet me in the bedroom at 7 pm. I will know it is you when there is a soft double tap on the door.

Just to be a bit bossy, you can also add to the text:

Set your alerts for this specific time or face severe consequences.

If your partner is as romantic as you are, he might respond with a kissy face emoji, or to be more enticing, a shocked face emoji to show how frightened he is of what you could do to him.

Can you imagine the anticipation building already?

The next step is to create a sensual environment with burning candles and soft music, then it's time to embody the alter ego that you have conceived for yourself. Become confident and sinfully sexy. Become the total opposite of your coy and introverted self. Spritz yourself with perfume because this ignites the sense of smell in your partner, which in turns gets him to notice every single part of the scene created for his pleasure.

When it is obvious that your partner might step into the room, you should be lying across the bed with your legs wide open! Make his first sight of you irresistible. Greet him with a scene of visual stimulation. He will be ready but you must slow him down.

The purpose of the background music is important. It should only be instrumental or of a jazzy nature, so that neither of you is distracted. Your partner's focus as well as yours ought to be on the vibe of the song, not its lyrics. Remember: the goal is to stimulate the mind. All your senses must be tuned in to ensure they stay the course, which leads to an intense orgasm.

Now let's get back to you. You should ooze sexiness. As much as I am tempted to tell you how to do that, the best way is to find what you perceive sexiness to look like and go with it. If your perception is a sexy piece of lingerie with a red-colored wig, go with that. Allow your alter ego to dress exactly as you have perceived her to be.

Think of yourself as a cherished, upscale, and confident woman that every man desires and you can get into the character without even becoming aware of it. Continue the thought by knowing that your partner is smiling because he feels lucky that he has you.

Understand the power of fantasizing and every single thought will become your reality.

Back to the main event—masturbation—you need to acquire a dildo that satisfies you. There are so many choices on the market, so there's no need to be scared. Start small, like a rabbit. Apart from your thumb (which could easily rub your clitoris and drive you to the climax of your fantasies), the dildo—however small—will stimulate the clitoris in such a way that will get your dripping with so much cum, you will wish for a rigid dick inside of you.

Instruct your partner to undress and take a seat. Get him to be patient—and this you can say with authority. Trust me, commanding your partner during sex is a major turn on since there are many people who appreciate a partner that takes charge of everything in the bedroom.

When he is obedient to your instructions, begin to touch yourself in a self-satisfying way. Slowly pull out your dildo and begin to tease yourself with it. Rub it against your clit and moan unashamedly. When you finally penetrate your pussy hole with two fingers, make sure your partner can hear the soft moan that accompanies it.

After the first orgasm, invite your partner to join you. It can only get better at this point and he can forever be reminded of this unusual-yet-totally-gratifying sex each time he looks at you.

Robot Head

Robot Head is just a lot of fun! Robots work on command and thus, for this technique to be executed, you must put your inner acting skills to work. Imagine that you were given a part in a movie to portray a robot. What would you look like? How would you act? Do you listen to every instruction and act accordingly, without a mind of your own?

In my own fantasy, I would like to be a flawless sex goddess with full lips and a perfectly round-shaped ass. Your fantasy might be different but keep in mind that the robot that we have agreed to become is solely for the purpose of giving blow jobs. Thus, it only acts on specific commands. You exist only to tease and stimulate your partner's sexual organ with your lips and tongue.

Keep the commands simple. Most commands are nonverbal, anyway. What does that mean? Simply put, hold your partner's dick and pull it confidently into your mouth. Your partner instinctively knows what to do. He knows how he should move slowly at first and penetrate every corner of your mouth. Afterwards, he will leave the next act to you, waiting patiently as you suckle hard or nibble softly.

Is your imagination there yet? It should be working overtime with these possibilities!

Be on your knees in front of your partner if you can. Your hands could be behind your back. This denotes that you are

ready to be submissive and that you can allow your partner to control how to receive pleasure by penetrating your mouth whichever way he desires. As a head robot, your mouth must be open in the right manner to receive an erect penis.

Yes! You can also text your partner how you want this to play out before he meets you. For instance, text him this:

I'm sending random words for a reason, so don't delete them. You'll need them later. Forehead, Right Cheek, Nose, Hair! You choose but don't overthink it. This is supposed to be fun, not a science project.

You can also write some commands to match the words sent in the earlier text on a sheet of paper:

Right Cheek = On

Nose = Deep throat

Forehead = Nut

Hair = Grab

Beneath the commands, explain to him that you are a robot. You can put it however you want but you can also borrow some or all of the following sentences for your excitement:

Love, note that Robot Head only works with the touch of your penis in my mouth. You must tap your penis to match only the commands provided. No deviation or it will not function properly as I want it to. Be aware that my battery life is only ten minutes, or until I get tired. You must taste me when the battery runs down!*

*Did you think I forgot about you in this equation? Think again. You need to get yours too!

In a nutshell, you can always switch it up and he can be the robot. This time, you can be the one to create the commands while you watch your partner follow them. By doing this, you become the sole controller of whatever both of you decide to do. You can tell your partner, for instance, to bury his head between your legs. Tell him to dig his tongue deep into your pleasure hole. Insist that he doesn't stop until you have your cum splattering all over his face.

As with all our Seduction Games, always keep it interesting. Give the robot a name. Make it an inside joke only you and your partner understand. Send random texts from time to time about it. "I changed the battery in Roberta!" you could say.

You know that will definitely put an instant smile on his face.

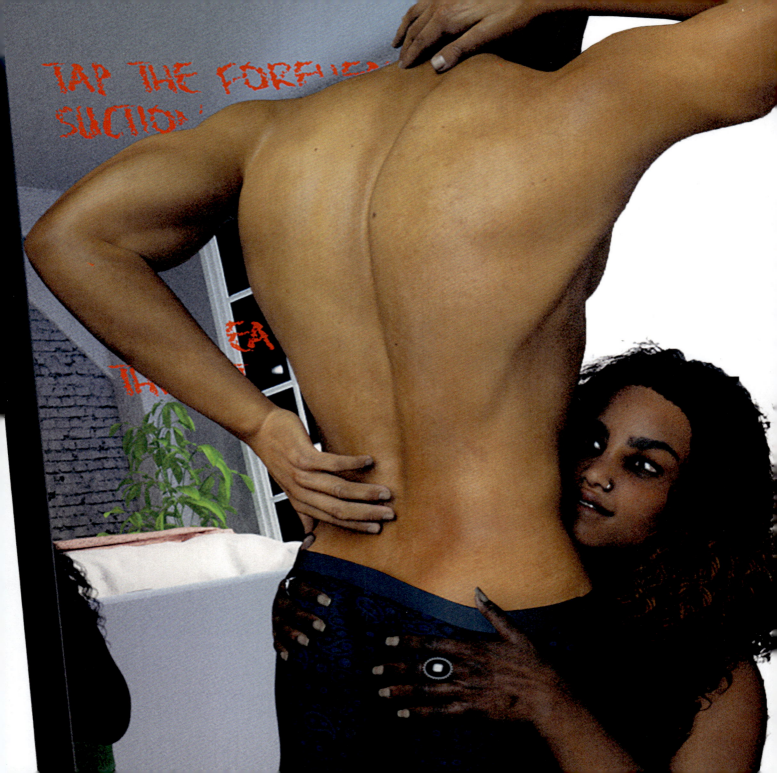

Cocktails And Porn

Yes, porn is good and it is not just for men. It is an excellent tool to stimulate your mind in order to reach a calculated orgasm. If you feel offended by this tool, then perhaps skip this chapter.

Rest assured, porn gets you aroused quicker than most dildos. Seeing others so shamelessly engrossed in each other's pleasure should excite you. It should make your breasts tingle in response to the throb between your legs.

The truth is that some people cannot handle real erotic movies. If this is the case for you, start with soft porn. This is a short or full movie clip that isn't too explicit with the sex act. It features only subtle romance scenes to stimulate your imagination and get you aroused, without you being fully conscious of it. I personally choose my porn carefully because I want to enjoy certain eye candy.

Think outside of the box when choosing porn. If there is something sexual you have been curious about, put that in a porn search engine and see what turns up. There is literally an unlimited amount of inspiration!

Also, have you ever tried watching porn together with your partner with the volume muted? This technique really sets a mood of sexual tension. You can relax together with cocktails and deserts. Chocolate is good since it melts easily when touched—an arousing food, don't you think?

As the porn plays, do well to take control of the performance. It may be impossible for your partner to take his eyes off what is happening on the screen, but not for long. You are in charge. You are both going to be your own porn stars, playing out your own script.

If the scene in the movie has the actress showing her ass and caressing it, then you should do the same—if not better. Ask your partner to spank you as you twerk your ass at him.

Soft taps should be out of it. Smacking is the real deal. It will excite you and you must moan and ask for another because you have had naughty thoughts that require a spanking.

Let this thought excite you. You can already imagine what could be going through his mind. Keep up with the scene and let your partner know that you are feeling freaky. Tell him that the time you spend together is only the beginning, providing he is willing to keep up…

Let The Games Begin

This guide is intended to get you started on a new path to a happier and fulfilling sex life. When you are not often satisfied sexually (what I call a "bedroom slump"), it creates an unhappy state of mind and that ultimately leads to an unhappy life.

You know your partner, so have that conversation that explains why you have decided to change…why you have decided to spice up both your desires, and then move onwards and upwards.

Whatever life stage you're at, don't give up on good sex and don't ever give up on being desired. Having both qualities is a basic human function, like blinking. Your body needs this active stimulation, so take care of it in every way. It is one of the reasons why masturbation is good for you, plus enjoying good sex can definitely lift your mood.

I'm going to finish by providing some sexy affirmations that you can use daily. Feel free to modify them to fit your unique needs.

I would say "good luck" but I don't think luck has anything to do with great sex! I believe the willingness to step out of your comfort zone and use your imagination is all that is needed to achieve that euphoric orgasm.

Sexy Daily Affirmations

I *deserve* an orgasm every **day**

I am amazingly *sexy*

I am *desired*

My Sexual Vibe is *contagious*

I *deserve* great sex

I am an unforgettable *lover*

There is no other *sex* like mine

Freaky
Notes

_____

_____

_____

_____

_____

_____

_____

_____

_____

For more from the Boudoir Boss please visit www.BoudoirBoss.com to join our mailing list for updates of new releases.
Follow the Boudoir Boss on social Media,
IG @boudoirbossy
Twitter: @boudoirbossy

48446175R10031

Made in the USA
Columbia, SC
08 January 2019